Even when everything goes wrong for Sara Crewe, she is determined to behave like 'a little princess'. Parted from her father who is in India, the little rich girl goes to a school run by the cruel Miss Minchin. There Sara makes friends and enemies as she becomes well known for her ability to 'pretend' and to make up stories. When she suddenly becomes very poor and is half starved and like a beggar-girl, it is Sara's imagination and her kindness which help her to find happiness again.

Written nearly a hundred years ago, this story has been retold and beautifully illustrated for young readers.

PERKS

British Library Cataloguing in Publication Data

Collins, Joan, *1917-*
    A Little Princess. — (Ladybird children's classics. Series 740)
    I. Title   II. Tourret, Shirley.
III. Burnett, Frances Hodgson. A Little Princess
823'.914[J]   PZ7
    ISBN 0-7214-0863-X

First edition

© LADYBIRD BOOKS LTD MCMLXXXV

A LITTLE PRINCESS

by Frances Hodgson Burnett
retold by Joan Collins
with illustrations by Shirley Tourret

Ladybird Books Loughborough

Sara

Sara Crewe was only seven years old. Her mother had died when she was born. Sara had always lived in India, with her father, an army captain, who was very rich. Now she was to go to school in England, and be parted from him.

"You'll be living in a house with lots of other girls," said her father, to cheer her up. "And when you're big and clever enough, you can come home and look after me!" But he knew he would be very lonely without his quaint old-fashioned little daughter.

Sara did not much care for other girls. She liked reading best, and making up stories, and

talking to her doll, Emily, who, she was sure, understood every word she said.

Captain Crewe had bought Sara lots of beautiful clothes — velvet dresses, trimmed with fur, petticoats with real lace frills, muffs, and a hat with a curling ostrich feather.

All this finery however did not make up to Sara for parting with her jolly, loving father. But she was a soldier's daughter, so she knew she had to be brave. "It's like going into battle!" she thought.

On a dark winter's day in London, Sara and her father set off through the foggy streets in a horse-drawn cab.

The cab drew up outside an ugly brick house, in a square. It had a brass plate on the door:

MISS MINCHIN
Select Seminary for Young Ladies

They were shown into a dark drawing room, with hard polished furniture, and a heavy marble clock on the mantelpiece.

"I don't like it!" whispered Sara, and her father squeezed her hand.

Then Miss Minchin came in. She was just like her house: tall, dull and ugly. She had large, cold, fishy eyes and a large, cold, fishy smile.

"What a beautiful child!" she gushed. (She said that to all the rich parents.)

Sara knew she was not beautiful. She did not have long golden curls and blue eyes. Her hair was short, dark and glossy, and she had a quaint little face, with enormous green eyes.

Captain Crewe had arranged for Sara to have her own sitting room, a French maid called Mariette, and all the books she wanted.

"She is very quick at learning," he explained. "But she must play, too, and I want her to have everything she needs to make her happy!" Then he said a sad goodbye to his little daughter.

Sara went straight up to her room and locked the door. She wanted to be alone, after parting with her father.

Miss Minchin and her plump sister, Miss Amelia, listened outside her door, but could hear no sound. "Why doesn't she cry, like the other children?" they wondered.

But that was not Sara's way.

The French Lesson

Next morning the pupils whispered together, as Sara, in her dark blue school dress, stood by Miss Minchin's desk.

"I don't think she's at all pretty!" sniffed Lavinia, one of the older girls, spitefully.

"Those green eyes make you look at her twice, though!" said her friend, Jessie.

"She's wearing a frilly petticoat! How ridiculous!" said the jealous Lavinia.

Sara stood there quietly. Miss Minchin gave her a list of French words to look at, until Monsieur Defarge the French master arrived. Sara knew all the words already. Her mother had been French, and so her father had often talked to Sara in that language. She tried to tell Miss Minchin so, but she would not listen.

Then Monsieur Defarge arrived.

"Your new pupil is being difficult. She does not wish to learn French!" said the cross Miss Minchin. "Her papa wishes her to learn it, for he has engaged a French maid for her!"

"I think he engaged Mariette because he thought I would *like* her!" said Sara.

"It is not a question of your likes and dislikes, young lady!" snapped Miss Minchin. "I can see you have been spoiled!"

Sara looked up at Monsieur Defarge with her innocent green eyes. She spoke politely in pretty and fluent French. She explained that she already knew the French words in the list. Monsieur Defarge was delighted with her.

"I cannot teach her anything," he said. "Her accent is perfect."

"Silence! Stop giggling, girls!" snapped Miss Minchin at the naughty class. "You should have told me, Sara!"

"I did try!" said Sara.

Miss Minchin began to dislike her new pupil.

Sara makes a friend

During the French lesson, Sara noticed a fat, plain little girl called Ermengarde, who was chewing the ribbon on the end of her pigtail. When she was asked to read, she pronounced the words very badly. Lavinia, Jessie and the others made fun of her.

Ermengarde's face went red, and tears came into her eyes. Sara was sorry for her, and wanted to be her friend. If she saw anyone in trouble, she always tried to help.

So when the lesson was over, she invited Ermengarde up to her sitting room to meet Emily. She let her hold the doll in her lap, and sat down on the hearth-rug to tell Ermengarde stories, about the wonderful things that dolls can do, when nobody else is in the room.

"Can Emily really walk and talk?" said Ermengarde, clutching the doll.

"I *pretend* she can," said Sara, "and that makes it seem real. Don't you ever pretend things?"

"I'm not clever enough," said Ermengarde. "But you are clever, aren't you?"

"I don't know," said Sara. Then she suddenly looked sad, remembering that her father used to call her 'a clever little puss'.

"Do you love your father more than anything else in the world?" she asked earnestly.

Ermengarde was rather afraid of her father. He was so clever that he could not understand how a child of his could be so stupid. "I don't see him very often," she answered. "He's always in the library, reading."

"I love mine more than anything in the world, ten times over. But he's gone away," said Sara.

"Lavinia and Jessie are 'best friends'," said Ermengarde timidly. "Would you have me for yours? I know you're the cleverest girl and I'm the stupidest – but I do like you!"

"I'm glad of that," smiled Sara, her face lighting up. "Yes, we will be friends – and I can help you with your French!"

The Favourite Pupil

If Sara had been a different girl, she could easily have been spoilt. Although Miss Minchin did not like her, she always praised her. She was afraid that Sara might write to tell her father if she was unhappy.

Lavinia was very jealous. Till Sara came, she had been the star pupil.

Lavinia bullied all the younger girls and made them afraid of her.

Sara was quite different. She was friendly and motherly. She was specially kind to a troublesome little girl called Lottie, who had no mother.

Sara never showed off, for, as she told Ermengarde, "A lot of nice things have happened to me by accident. I was lucky to have a father who gave me everything I wanted. I can't help being good-tempered. For all I know, I may be horrid underneath. No one will ever know, because I never have any trials to test me."

"Lavinia hasn't any trials," said Ermengarde, "and she is horrid all the time."

Lavinia told Jessie, "There is nothing very grand about Sara's father being an Indian Army officer and those 'pretend' stories she makes up, about the tiger skin rug in her room coming alive, are just silly!"

What made Sara most popular was this gift for telling stories. When she sat in the middle of a circle of children, and began to invent the most wonderful things, her green eyes shone with excitement. She waved her hands, and raised or dropped her voice thrillingly, and made her stories of kings and queens and fairies all seem real.

"When I'm telling it, it doesn't seem made up!" she said. "I feel as if I am all the people in the story, one after the other!"

Becky

There was someone who thought Sara's stories were the most wonderful in the world. Her name was Becky. She was a poor little servant girl, who always had a smudge on her face. She blacked the shoes and the grates, scrubbed the floors, and carried the heavy coal scuttles up and down the stairs. Becky was ordered about by everybody from morning till night.

She used to take as long as she could to sweep the hearth in Sara's sitting room, just to listen to the stories.

"The mermaids swam softly about in the clear, green water, and dragged a fishing net

after them, woven of deep sea pearls,'' Sara was saying one day, in her soft voice. ''The princess sat on the white rocks and watched them.''

Becky sat back on her heels and dropped her brush in wonder. The voice of the story-teller drew her with it, into deep sea caves, paved with golden sand, where the light was a soft blue, and far away voices sang...

''That girl's been listening!'' cried Lavinia, sharply.

''Why shouldn't she?'' asked Sara.

''She's only a servant!'' sneered Lavinia.

After that, Sara often used to talk to Becky. She gave her cake and made her sit by the

fire, and told her the rest of the story about the mermaids and the princess.

"I think *you're* just like a princess!" said Becky, shyly.

"I've often wondered what it was like to be a princess," said Sara thoughtfully. "Perhaps I'll pretend to be one!"

Becky was often hungry, so Sara used to buy little meat pies for her, and smuggle them indoors in her muff. Becky would go back to the cold attic where she slept, much comforted by the pies, but even more by Sara's friendship.

The Diamond Mines

There was exciting news for Sara from her father one day. He had joined with a friend to buy some diamond mines. This sounded like a fairy tale to Sara. She told the girls stories about mysterious underground passages, glittering with precious stones.

Lavinia said, "I don't believe it! It's just one of her 'pretends'!"

Jessie said, "One of her new 'pretends' is that she's a princess! Lottie told me. Fancy that!"

Just then Sara came into the room. She was upset to find that they knew her precious secret. "It's true," she said, with dignity. "I do pretend I'm a princess, so that I can try to behave like one!"

Time went on, and it was Sara's eleventh birthday. Her father had sent her a wonderful French doll. "It will be my last doll," Sara wrote to him. "I'm almost grown up now."

Her father did not write so excitedly about the diamond mines this time. "Business gives me a headache," he said.

Sara had another present she treasured. It was from Becky, who had made it herself. It was a grubby pin cushion made out of red flannel. Black pins spelled out the words on it. "Menny hapy returns."

"I knew you could 'pretend' it was satin with diamond pins," said Becky. "I did, when I was a-making it!"

Sara's Birthday Party

There was to be a party for the whole school, and Sara asked if Becky could come. Miss Minchin had to agree, but she did not like it.

"Go and stand in the corner," she commanded, "not too near the young ladies."

Becky did not mind, as long as she could see the presents.

"Sara is going to be very rich one day," Miss Minchin went on. "That is why her father placed her in my care, to be educated properly. She has kindly asked you all to her party, so you must thank her. Now I will leave you to enjoy yourselves," and she swept out, importantly.

The girls all rushed to look at the presents, especially the Last Doll. She was gorgeous, and had a trunk full of dresses and jewels.

"She's almost as big as Lottie!" gasped one little girl.

"Do you suppose she understands what we are saying?" said Sara.

"You're always supposing things," said Lavinia. "It's all very well when you have everything you want. Could you 'pretend' if you were a beggar in an attic?"

Sara was thoughtful. "I believe I could. If I were a beggar, I would have to pretend all the time. But it mightn't be easy!"

Just at this moment, Miss Amelia came into the room. "You must all go and have tea!" she fluttered. "Mr Barrow, Sara's father's solicitor, has called, and Miss Minchin will see him in this room."

Everybody hurried out eagerly, and Miss Minchin entered, followed by a tall gentleman in a dark coat.

The Diamond Mines Again

Mr Barrow looked at the Last Doll and her wardrobe crossly. ''He certainly knew how to spend money!'' he remarked.

''He can afford it, of course!'' smiled Miss Minchin. ''Think of the diamond mines!''

''There are no diamond mines!'' said Mr Barrow, sharply. ''There never were. His friend cheated him, and ran away. The late Captain Crewe...''

''The late Captain Crewe? What do you mean?''

"He's dead, ma'am. Died of jungle fever and business worries, calling out for his little daughter. He didn't leave a penny!"

"Do you mean to tell me that Sara's a beggar? That she is left on my hands?" gasped Miss Minchin.

"She hasn't a relation or a penny in the world," said Mr Barrow grimly.

"But I have paid for all the presents and the party, since the last cheque came! I shall turn her out into the street!" cried Miss Minchin, indignantly.

"I should not advise that, ma'am. Think of the good name of the school! Better keep her and make use of her. She's a clever child." Mr Barrow bowed himself out, and shut the door.

Miss Minchin was furious. She called Miss Amelia. "Captain Crewe is dead. He died penniless and has left his spoiled child on my hands. Put a stop to this ridiculous party! Tell Sara to change her frock at once and put on a black one."

"Must I go and tell her? Now? In the middle of the party?" panted Miss Amelia, who was kinder than her sister. But she did not dare to argue, and crept out of the room, dabbing her eyes with her handkerchief.

A Different World

When Miss Amelia told Sara about her father, she did not make a sound. She just stood looking up at her, with big green eyes and a white face. Then she went up to her room and locked the door. She walked up and down, saying over and over again, in a queer, dull voice, "My papa is dead! My papa is dead!"

She told her doll Emily, "Papa is dead. He died in India, thousands of miles away."

She put on an old black frock that was too short for her, and tied her hair with a black ribbon. Then she went to Miss Minchin's room, carrying Emily.

"You will have no time for dolls now," said Miss Minchin coldly. "You are a beggar like Becky now, and must work for your living."

"Can I work?" said Sara, eagerly. "If I can work, it will not be so hard to bear."

"Yes, you can make yourself useful. You can help with the younger children, and run errands and work in the kitchen. Now go!"

Sara went up to her room. Miss Amelia was at the door. "You can't go in, Sara," she said, unhappily. "This isn't your room any more!"

"Where is my room?"

"Up in the attic, next to Becky's."

Sara climbed the shabby stairs that led to the top of the house. She opened the attic door and looked in. It was a different world.

The room had a slanting roof. The
whitewashed walls were peeling. There
was a rusty grate, an iron bedstead, with
a hard mattress, a few bits of old furniture,
and a red footstool, under a dirty skylight. All
she could see through it was a slate roof and
chimney pots.

Sara sat on the footstool with Emily in her
arms, and put her face down on the doll's
hair. She did not make a single sound.

After a while, there came a tap at the door, and an anxious little white face peeped in. It was Becky.

"Oh, Becky!" Sara cried. "I told you we were just the same as each other, just two little girls. You see it's true now. I'm not a princess any more!"

Becky ran to her and hugged her, sobbing. "Yes, Miss, you are!" she cried. "Whatever happens, you'll be a princess all the same! Nothing couldn't make you no different!"

Sara's New Life

Sara never forgot her first night in the attic, in the dark. She lay on her cold, hard bed and listened to the wind howling outside, and the rats scratching behind the walls.

Next day she was told to have her meals in the kitchen. She was to teach the younger girls French, but she was not allowed to talk to the other girls any more, nor have lessons with them. The cook and the housemaids ordered her about.

From being a small 'royal' personage, she became a shabby little servant, looking very queer as she grew out of her dresses. She worked hard to show that she was trying to earn her living. She ran errands in the rain and snow, did housework and all the odd jobs. She was often hungry, and nobody said a kind word to her. Becky was her only friend.

Sara was so miserable that she no longer believed that Emily understood what she said. "You're only a doll!" she cried, and threw her on the floor.

Ermengarde had been away from school when all this happened. When she came back, she could not understand why Sara looked so different, or why she passed her by in the passages without speaking. One night she found her way up the attic stairs.

"Oh Sara, I've missed you so!" she cried. "I thought you'd forgotten me! How can you bear living up in this horrid attic?"

"I can, if I pretend it's another place," said Sara. Her imagination began to work, for the first time since her troubles began. "I shall pretend I'm a prisoner in the Bastille!" she said. "I have been here for years and everyone has forgotten about me. Miss Minchin is the jailer and Becky – Becky is the prisoner in the next cell! I shall make friends with one of the rats and feed it crumbs!"

She turned to Ermengarde, her eyes shining, quite like the old Sara. "I shall 'pretend' and it will be a great comfort!"

The Large Family

Sara showed Ermengarde the view over the rooftops. The next door attic was empty. ''I wish someone would come and live there,'' said Sara, wistfully.

There was one house in the Square where a Large Family lived, with a sweet-faced mother, a jolly father, and several children. One day, one of the boys saw Sara, standing on the pavement, in her shabby frock and hat. She looked as if she was hungry. He found a sixpence in his pocket. ''Here you are, little girl,'' he said. ''Buy yourself something to eat!''

Sara realised with a shock she looked just like the poor little children she used to see on the pavements in her better days.

The mother of the Large Family said, ''Donald, why did you offer that girl money? I'm sure she isn't a beggar! Was she angry?''

''No, she said it was sweet of me!''

''A beggar wouldn't say that,'' said the mother thoughtfully.

After that, the Large Family were interested
in Sara, and watched her go by on her
errands. They called her 'the little-girl-who-
isn't-a-beggar'.

Once Sara had another piece of luck. She found a silver sixpence in the muddy street. She went into a nearby bun shop to see if anyone had lost it, and the bun-woman kindly gave her six hot buns for herself. Sara was hungry, but she saw a poor little girl outside in the gutter, and gave her five of them. "I think that is what a princess would do," she said to herself.

The Indian Gentleman

One day a furniture van came to the empty house next door. Sara watched the men carry in Eastern carpets, carved furniture, embroidered tapestries, and a figure of the god Buddha. "Somebody in that house must have lived in India," she thought.

The father of the Large Family seemed to be in charge, telling the workmen what to do.

Becky came up from the kitchen. "It's a Nindian gentleman!" she said excitedly. "He's very rich, but he's ill and the gentleman from the Large Family is his lawyer!"

Next day the Indian gentleman arrived, with a nurse and two menservants with turbans. He was not an Indian gentleman really, but an Englishman called Mr Carrisford who had lived in India. The servants at Miss Minchin's found out all about him.

"He lost all his money and the shock gave him brain fever," they said. "But now he's got it all back – something to do with mines."

"That's like what happened to Papa," said Sara, sadly.

One evening Sara was watching the pink and gold colours of the sunset over the rooftops, when she heard a squeaking noise from the attic opposite. She saw a dark face with gleaming eyes, topped by a snow-white turban, looking out. It was an Indian manservant, holding a chattering little monkey at the window.

Sara smiled, and he smiled back, letting go of the monkey. It scrambled over the roof and jumped up on Sara's shoulder.

She spoke in Hindustani. "Can you come and fetch him?"

Ram Dass was surprised and delighted to hear his own language spoken. He called Sara "Missie Sahib", speaking politely and respectfully, as her father's servants used to do.

Then he climbed over and collected the monkey, salaaming to Sara. He told her about his master who was so ill, but loved the cheeky monkey, because it made him laugh.

After he had gone, Sara felt more cheerful. "I can still be like a princess inside," she thought. "Just like Marie Antoinette in prison."

Ram Dass went to tell his master, Mr Carrisford, about the little servant in the cold bare attic. "She speaks like a noble child!" he said, wonderingly.

Mr Carrisford was sitting in his study, talking to Mr Carmichael, the father of the Large Family.

"Here we sit in comfort," he cried, "while poor little wretches live in misery! I wonder what has happened to Captain Crewe's little daughter? I hope she does not have to suffer like that, when I have all her father's money to give her!"

"If only her father had known the diamond mines were successful after all!" said his lawyer friend.

"She may be at school in Paris," said Mr Carrisford, hopefully. "Her mother was French. Perhaps we shall hear news of her soon."

The two gentlemen did not guess that the child they had been looking for, for so long, was just on the other side of the wall.

The Magic

Sara and Becky came up to the attic the next night, cold and hungry. Cook was cross and would not give them any supper. When Ermengarde heard this, she brought some cake, fruit and sweets that her aunt had sent her. Sara spread an old shawl on the table and put out her toothmug. (She had no cups.) Then she lit a piece of paper in the grate to look like a fire.

Her eyes shone with the old glow. She forgot the cold streets outside. "It's a magic feast!" she said.

But just then, heavy footsteps stamped up
the stairs. Miss Minchin had found out!
Lavinia had told her! She swept up the feast
and sent Becky to her attic. Sara stared at her.

"Why are you looking like that?" asked
Miss Minchin.

"I was just wondering," said Sara, "what
my father would say if he knew where I am
tonight."

"Rude, naughty child!" Miss Minchin
screamed, and stamped down the stairs,
pushing Ermengarde in front of her.

Sara crept into her hard bed and tried to bear what had happened. "Suppose," she thought, "there really was a big, bright fire in the grate..." and she fell asleep, 'supposing'.

While she was asleep, two dark figures entered and moved silently about the room.

When Sara woke up, she thought she was still dreaming. She was covered with warm blankets. There *was* a blazing fire, and rosy lamplight in the room. Her table was laid with a white cloth and dishes. There was a cosy

dressing-gown and slippers. It was the room
of her dreams!

On the table was a note. "To the little girl in
the attic, from – a friend."

Becky woke up to see the Princess Sara as she remembered her, standing by her bed, in a rich crimson robe.

"Oh, Becky, come and see!" she cried. "It's magic!"

The Visitor

The next day a parcel was delivered for Sara. It was full of warm clothing, shoes, dresses and a beautiful coat.

Miss Minchin was worried. Could a rich relative have found out how Sara was being treated? When Miss Minchin had thought about it for a while, she allowed Sara to come back and have lessons with the other girls.

"My word!" said Jessie. "Look at Princess Sara! Someone must have left her a large fortune!"

"I wish I could thank whoever is doing it!" thought Sara.

That night the little monkey came to the attic window, cold and frightened. "Come in with me, darling," said Sara. "I'll take you back to the Indian gentleman in the morning."

The Other Side of the Wall

Next day Mr Carrisford sat in his library, feeling miserable. There was no news of Captain Crewe's daughter in Paris. The mother of the Large Family had brought her children to cheer him up.

"Did you tell Mr Carrisford about the little-girl-who-isn't-a-beggar?" said Donald. "The one I gave sixpence to?"

Just then Ram Dass came in. "Sahib," he said, "the child I told you of is here. Would you like to see her?"

Sara came in, carrying the chattering monkey. "Shall I give him to Ram Dass?" she asked, and spoke to him in Hindustani.

"How do you know Hindustani?" asked Mr Carrisford, surprised.

"I was born in India, I was sent here to school, but my father died and there was no money. So now I am a servant."

"How did he lose his money?"

"He trusted his friend too much."

Mr Carrisford looked startled. "What was his name?"

"Ralph Crewe. He died in India."

"Carmichael..." gasped Mr Carrisford. "It is the child!"

"What child?" said Sara, bewildered.

"Mr Carrisford was your father's friend," explained Mr Carmichael. "We have been looking for you for two years!"

"And all the time I was next door!" said Sara. "Just the other side of the wall!"

Sara forgave Mr Carrisford when she heard how ill he had been, and how he had looked for her everywhere, and how he and Ram Dass had made the Magic in the attic.

Mr Carrisford already looked much better, now that "Missie Sahib" was going to live with them. Ram Dass and the monkey were happy, too!

The only one who was not happy was Miss Minchin. Even Miss Amelia turned against her, and some of the parents took their children away from the school.

Becky was to live with Sara. Ram Dass went over to the attic for the last time to tell her. Becky could hardly believe it.

One day Sara and Mr Carrisford called at the bun shop. There was the little beggar-girl, neat and well fed, serving the buns. The bun-woman had taken the girl in to help in the shop and the kitchen.

"Could you give her some money," said Sara to Mr Carrisford, "to give buns to hungry children? Because she knows what it is to be hungry, too."

The little girl looked after Sara as she went out of the shop and drove away. "She's just like a little princess," she said.